Our Emotions and Behavior

I Don't Want to Wait!

Sue Graves

Illustrated by Emanuela Carletti
and Desideria Guicciardini

free spirit
PUBLISHING®

Maisy was **never patient.**
She hated waiting for her birthday even when it was far away!

At school, she **wouldn't wait** patiently to see Miss Lu even though there were others ahead of her in line.

Maisy hated waiting for her turn to talk during sharing time. She always interrupted others when they were speaking. Miss Lu said it was **rude to interrupt**.

When Maisy got impatient, she got mad. She **shouted and yelled** over other people so no one could hear what they were saying.

One day, Miss Lu said everyone was going to make animal masks. She said all the children should paint them **carefully**. She said they would need to wait patiently for the paint to dry.

4

But Maisy **didn't wait** patiently. She didn't wait for the paint to dry at all. The paint dripped all over her. Miss Lu was angry.

That afternoon after school, Raffi came over to play. He brought his new game. He told Maisy they had to **take turns** rolling the dice.

But Maisy didn't want to wait for her turn. She **grabbed the dice** from Raffi. Raffi was upset.

That Saturday, Maisy's big sister, Lola, was coming to stay. Maisy loved Lola. She was a lot of fun. But Lola called to say her bus **was late**.

8

Mom said Maisy would have to **wait patiently** for her sister to arrive. Maisy scowled and tapped her foot.

Lola arrived later that afternoon.
Maisy wanted to play with her right away.
But Lola said she wanted to talk with
Mom first. She said she'd play with Maisy
after that.

Maisy got very **angry**.
She stomped upstairs to her bedroom
and **slammed the door**.

After a while, Maisy calmed down.
She wished she hadn't stomped her feet.
She wished she hadn't slammed the door.

She went to find Lola.

13

Maisy told her sister she was sorry. Lola said everyone feels impatient sometimes. She told Maisy she felt impatient when her bus was late, so she took **a deep breath** and thought about other things. She said that helped her feel better.

Maisy said that if she felt impatient again, maybe she could take a deep breath and **think about other things** too.

The next day, Lola and Maisy went to the park. Maisy ran to the slide, but Raffi had gotten there first. He was going down the slide very, very **slowly**.

Maisy took **a deep breath**.
She looked for shapes in the clouds.
She waited patiently for her turn.

Then Lola said it was time for ice cream. But the ice cream man was very busy. Maisy had to **wait patiently** at the end of the line. She counted all the different flavors.

She even made up some of her own!

At last, it was Maisy's turn. The man said she had waited very patiently. He gave her an extra scoop of ice cream for being so patient. Maisy said it was

much nicer to be patient!

Can you tell the story of what happened when George and his dad baked a cake?

How do you think George felt when his cake wasn't ready? How did he feel at the end of the story?

A note about sharing this book

The **Our Emotions and Behavior** series has been developed to provide a starting point for further discussion on children's feelings and behavior, in relation both to themselves and to other people.

I Don't Want to Wait!
This story explores in a reassuring way the importance of being patient and understanding that not everything can happen immediately—and as it turns out, realizing that some things are worth waiting for.

The book aims to encourage children to have a developing awareness of behavioral expectations in different settings. It also invites children to begin to consider the consequences of their words and actions for themselves and others.

Picture story
The picture story on pages 22 and 23 provides an opportunity for speaking and listening. Children are encouraged to tell the story illustrated in the panels: George and his dad are baking a cake, and George doesn't want to wait for it to bake. He asks his dad to take the cake out of the oven too early and the cake collapses. On the next attempt, George is more patient and the cake comes out perfectly.

How to use the book
The book is designed for adults to share with either an individual child or a group of children as a starting point for discussion.

The book also provides visual support and repeated words and phrases to build confidence in children who are starting to read on their own.

Before reading the story
Choose a time to read when you and the children are relaxed and have time to share the story.

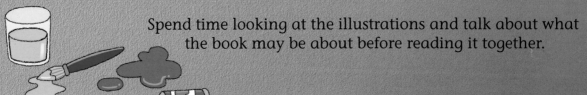

Spend time looking at the illustrations and talk about what the book may be about before reading it together.

After reading, talk about the book with the children

- What was the book about? Have the children ever been impatient while waiting for an exciting event to happen? Examples might be a birthday or a special party. How did they feel? Did it seem to them that time passed slowly when they especially wanted something to happen?

- Have children ever rushed through a task and spoiled the outcome due to being impatient? Invite children to share their experiences.

- As a group, talk about why it is important to be patient when, for example, playing a game. Why can being impatient spoil a game for others? Extend this by talking about the importance of waiting your turn in class, either to talk in group time or to ask for the teacher's attention. Encourage children to take turns speaking and to listen politely while others are talking.

- Look at the picture story and talk about what is happening. Invite children to act out the story. Discuss performances afterward as a group.

- Talk about being patient in school. Explain that being part of a school community requires some patience. For instance, a teacher may be busy helping another child.

- Discuss the idea that waiting for your turn in a game is necessary for the game to be played successfully.

- Look at the end of the story together and talk about the way Maisy takes her mind off waiting by thinking about other things. Ask children to write or draw things they could think about while they have to wait for something. Make a display of their work.

25

To Isabelle, William A., George, William G., Max, Emily, Leo, Caspar, Felix, and Phoebe—S.G.

Published in North America by Free Spirit Publishing Inc., Minneapolis, Minnesota, 2019

Library of Congress Cataloging-in-Publication Data
Names: Graves, Sue, 1950– author. | Carletti, Emanuela, illustrator. | Guicciardini, Desideria, illustrator.
Title: I don't want to wait! / Sue Graves ; illustrated by Emanuela Carletti and Desideria Guicciardini.
Description: Minneapolis : Free Spirit Publishing Inc., [2019] | Series: Our emotions and behavior | Audience: Age: 4–8.
Identifiers: LCCN 2018020685| ISBN 9781631984136 (hardcover) | ISBN 1631984136 (hardcover)
Subjects: LCSH: Patience—Juvenile literature. | Conduct of life—Juvenile literature.
Classification: LCC BJ1533.P3 G73 2019 | DDC 179/.9—dc23 LC record available at https://lccn.loc.gov/2018020685

Reading Level Grade 2; Interest Level Ages 4–8 ; Fountas & Pinnell Guided Reading Level L

10 9 8 7 6 5 4 3 2 1
Printed in China
H13771018

Free Spirit Publishing Inc.
6325 Sandburg Road, Suite 100
Minneapolis, MN 55427-3674
(612) 338-2068
help4kids@freespirit.com
www.freespirit.com

First published in 2019 by Franklin Watts, an imprint of Hachette Children's Books • London, UK, and Sydney, Australia

Text © The Watts Publishing Group 2019
Illustrations © Emanuela Carletti and Desideria Guicciardini 2019

The rights of Sue Graves to be identified as the author and Emanuela Carletti and Desideria Guicciardini as the illustrators of this Work have been asserted in accordance with the Copyright, Designs and Patents Act, 1988.

Editor: Jackie Hamley
Designer: Peter Scoulding